$10.⁸⁰

Marmalade's Snowy Day

by Cindy Wheeler

Alfred A. Knopf · New York

FOR MEMAW
AND GRAND DADDY

This is a Borzoi Book published by Alfred A. Knopf, Inc.

Copyright © 1982 by Cindy Wheeler

Manufactured in the United States of America
2   4   6   8   10   9   7   5   3   1

Library of Congress Cataloging in Publication Data
Wheeler, Cindy. Marmalade's snowy day.
Summary: Marmalade looks for a warm place to hide from the snow outside.
[1. Cats—Fiction. 2. Snow—Fiction] I. Title.
PZ7.W5593Marf   [E]   81-20867
ISBN 0-394-85025-4   AACR2   ISBN 0-394-95025-9 (lib. bdg.)

13763 E

It is snowing.

The sky is white.

The ground is white.

Marmalade finds a warm spot.

Not for long!

Everyone is going out.

Marmalade goes out, too.

The snow is cold.

Watch out, Marmalade!

Marmalade does not want to play.

Marmalade finds a place to hide.

But not for long!

Here, snowman.

Marmalade's feet are cold.

Marmalade wants to go home.

Here we go!

All right, Marmalade.

A warm place...at last!

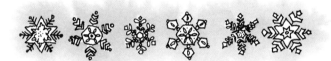

Cindy Wheeler grew up in Alabama, Virginia, and North Carolina. After receiving a B.F.A. degree from Auburn University, Ms. Wheeler worked for a bookseller and for a publisher. Now she devotes full time to writing and illustrating children's books.

Ms. Wheeler lives in Garrison, New York, with her husband and one black cat.